FOR JOAN, TO READ TO BABY

Pussy-cat sits by the fire –
How should she be fair?
In walks the little dog –
Says "Pussy are you there?
How do you do Mistress Pussy?
Mistress Pussy, how do you do?"
"I thank you kindly little dog,
I fare as well as you!"

OLD RHYME

FREDERICK WARNE

Published by the Penguin Group
Registered office: 80 Strand, London, WC2R ORL
Penguin Young Readers Group, 345 Hudson Street, New York, N.Y. 10014, USA

First published 1905 by Frederick Warne
This edition with new reproductions of Beatrix Potter's book illustrations first published 2007
This edition copyright © Frederick Warne & Co. 2007
New reproductions of Beatrix Potter's book illustrations copyright © Frederick Warne & Co. 2002
Original copyright in text and illustrations © Frederick Warne & Co., 1905

Frederick Warne & Co. is the owner of all rights, copyrights and trademarks
in the Beatrix Potter character names and illustrations.

Manufactured in China

THE TALE OF
THE PIE AND THE PATTY-PAN

BY BEATRIX POTTER

FREDERICK WARNE

ONCE upon a time there was a Pussy-cat called
Ribby, who invited a little dog called Duchess,
to tea.

"Come in good time, my dear Duchess," said
Ribby's letter, "and we will have something so very
very nice. I am baking it in a pie-dish — a pie-dish
with a pink rim. You never tasted anything so
good! And *you* shall eat it all! *I* will eat muffins,
my dear Duchess!" wrote Ribby.

Duchess read the letter and wrote an answer:
"I will come with much pleasure at a quarter past
four. But it is very strange. *I* was just going to
invite you to come here, to supper, my dear Ribby,
to eat something *most delicious*.

"I will come very punctually, my dear Ribby,"
wrote Duchess; and then at the end she added —
"I hope it isn't mouse?"

And then she thought that did not look quite
polite; so she scratched out "isn't mouse" and
changed it to "I hope it will be fine," and she
gave her letter to the postman.

BUT she thought a great deal about Ribby's pie, and she read Ribby's letter over and over again.

"I am dreadfully afraid it *will* be mouse!" said Duchess to herself — "I really couldn't, *couldn't* eat mouse pie. And I shall have to eat it, because it is a party. And *my* pie was going to be veal and ham. A pink and white pie-dish! and so is mine; just like Ribby's dishes; they were both bought at Tabitha Twitchit's."

Duchess went into her larder and took the pie off a shelf and looked at it.

"It is all ready to put into the oven. Such lovely pie-crust; and I put in a little tin patty-pan to hold up the crust; and I made a hole in the middle with a fork to let out the steam — Oh I do wish I could eat my own pie, instead of a pie made of mouse!"

9

DUCHESS considered and considered and read Ribby's letter again —

"A pink and white pie-dish — and *you* shall eat it *all*. 'You' means me — then Ribby is not going to even taste the pie herself? A pink and white pie-dish! Ribby is sure to go out to buy the muffins ... Oh what a good idea! Why shouldn't I rush along and put my pie into Ribby's oven when Ribby isn't there?"

Duchess was quite delighted with her own cleverness!

Ribby in the meantime had received Duchess's answer, and as soon as she was sure that the little dog could come — she popped *her* pie into the oven.

THERE were two ovens, one above the other; some other knobs and handles were only ornamental and not intended to open. Ribby put the pie into the lower oven; the door was very stiff.

"The top oven bakes too quickly," said Ribby to herself. "It is a pie of the most delicate and tender mouse minced up with bacon. And I have taken out all the bones; because Duchess did nearly choke herself with a fish-bone last time I gave a party. She eats a little fast — rather big mouthfuls. But a most genteel and elegant little dog; infinitely superior company to Cousin Tabitha Twitchit."

RIBBY put on some coal and swept up the hearth. Then she went out with a can to the well, for water to fill up the kettle.

Then she began to set the room in order, for it was the sitting-room as well as the kitchen. She shook the mats out at the front door and put them straight; the hearth-rug was a rabbit-skin. She dusted the clock and the ornaments on the mantelpiece, and she polished and rubbed the tables and chairs.

Then she spread a very clean white tablecloth, and set out her best china tea-set, which she took out of a wall-cupboard near the fire-place. The tea-cups were white with a pattern of pink roses; and the dinner-plates were white and blue.

When Ribby had laid the table she took a jug and a blue and white dish, and went out down the field to the farm, to fetch milk and butter.

WHEN she came back, she peeped into the bottom oven; the pie looked very comfortable.

Ribby put on her shawl and bonnet and went out again with a basket, to the village shop to buy a packet of tea, a pound of lump sugar, and a pot of marmalade.

And just at the same time, Duchess came out of *her* house, at the other end of the village.

RIBBY met Duchess half-way down the street, also carrying a basket, covered with a cloth. They only bowed to one another; they did not speak, because they were going to have a party.

As soon as Duchess had got round the corner out of sight — she simply ran! Straight away to Ribby's house!

RIBBY went into the shop and bought what she required, and came out, after a pleasant gossip with Cousin Tabitha Twitchit.

Cousin Tabitha was disdainful afterwards in conversation —

"A little *dog* indeed! Just as if there were no CATS in Sawrey! And a *pie* for afternoon tea! The very idea!" said Cousin Tabitha Twitchit.

RIBBY went on to Timothy Baker's and bought
the muffins. Then she went home. There seemed
to be a sort of scuffling noise in the back passage,
as she was coming in at the front door.

"I trust that is not that Pie; the spoons are
locked up, however," said Ribby.

But there was nobody there. Ribby opened
the bottom oven door with some difficulty,
and turned the pie. There began to be a pleasing
smell of baked mouse!

DUCHESS in the meantime, had slipped out at the back door.

"It is a very odd thing that Ribby's pie was *not* in the oven when I put mine in! And I can't find it anywhere; I have looked all over the house. I put *my* pie into a nice hot oven at the top. I could not turn any of the other handles; I think that they

are all shams," said Duchess, "but I wish I could have removed the pie made of mouse! I cannot think what she has done with it? I heard Ribby coming and I had to run out by the back door!"

DUCHESS went home and brushed her beautiful
black coat; and then she picked a bunch of flowers
in her garden as a present for Ribby; and passed
the time until the clock struck four.

RIBBY — having assured herself by careful search that there was really no one hiding in the cupboard or in the larder — went upstairs to change her dress.

She put on a lilac silk gown, for the party, and an embroidered muslin apron and tippet.

"It is very strange," said Ribby, "I did not *think* I left that drawer pulled out; has somebody been trying on my mittens?"

She came downstairs again, and made the tea, and put the teapot on the hob. She peeped again into the *bottom* oven; the pie had become a lovely brown, and it was steaming hot.

SHE sat down before the fire to wait for the little dog. "I am glad I used the *bottom* oven," said Ribby, "the top one would certainly have been very much too hot. I wonder why that cupboard door was open? Can there really have been someone in the house?"

Very punctually at four o'clock, Duchess started to go to the party. She ran so fast through the village that she was too early, and she had to wait a little while in the lane that leads down to Ribby's house.

"I wonder if Ribby has taken *my* pie out of the oven yet?" said Duchess, "and whatever can have become of the other pie made of mouse?"

AT a quarter past four to the minute, there came a most genteel little tap-tappity. "Is Mrs. Ribston at home?" inquired Duchess in the porch.

"Come in! and how do you do? my dear Duchess," cried Ribby. "I hope I see you well?"

"Quite well, I thank you, and how do *you* do, my dear Ribby?" said Duchess. "I've brought you some flowers; what a delicious smell of pie!"

"Oh, what lovely flowers! Yes, it is mouse and bacon!"

"DO not talk about food, my dear Ribby," said Duchess; "what a lovely white tea-cloth! . . . Is it done to a turn? Is it still in the oven?"

"I think it wants another five minutes," said Ribby. "Just a shade longer; I will pour out the tea, while we wait. Do you take sugar, my dear Duchess?"

"Oh yes, please! my dear Ribby; and may I have a lump upon my nose?"

"With pleasure, my dear Duchess; how beautifully you beg! Oh, how sweetly pretty!"

Duchess sat up with the sugar on her nose and sniffed —

"How good that pie smells! I do love veal and ham — I mean to say mouse and bacon —"

SHE dropped the sugar in confusion, and had
to go hunting under the tea-table, so she did not
see which oven Ribby opened in order to get
out the pie.

Ribby set the pie upon the table; there was a
very savoury smell.

DUCHESS came out from under the tablecloth munching sugar, and sat up on a chair.

"I will first cut the pie for you; I am going to have muffin and marmalade," said Ribby.

"Do you really prefer muffin? Mind the patty-pan!"

"I beg your pardon?" said Ribby.

"May I pass you the marmalade?" said Duchess hurriedly.

THE pie proved extremely toothsome, and the muffins light and hot. They disappeared rapidly, especially the pie!

"I think" — (thought the Duchess to herself) — "I *think* it would be wiser if I helped myself to pie; though Ribby did not seem to notice anything when she was cutting it. What very small fine pieces it has cooked into! I did not remember that I had minced it up so fine; I suppose this is a quicker oven than my own."

"HOW fast Duchess is eating!" thought Ribby to herself, as she buttered her fifth muffin.

The pie-dish was emptying rapidly! Duchess had had four helps already, and was fumbling with the spoon.

"A little more bacon, my dear Duchess?" said Ribby.

"Thank you, my dear Ribby; I was only feeling for the patty-pan."

"THE patty-pan? my dear Duchess?"

"The patty-pan that held up the pie-crust," said Duchess, blushing under her black coat.

"Oh, I didn't put one in, my dear Duchess," said Ribby; "I don't think that it is necessary in pies made of mouse."

Duchess fumbled with the spoon — "I can't find it!" she said anxiously.

"There isn't a patty-pan," said Ribby, looking perplexed.

"Yes, indeed, my dear Ribby; where can it have gone to?" said Duchess.

"THERE most certainly is not one, my dear
Duchess. I disapprove of tin articles in puddings
and pies. It is most undesirable — (especially
when people swallow in lumps!)" she added in
a lower voice.

Duchess looked very much alarmed, and
continued to scoop the inside of the pie-dish.

"MY Great-aunt Squintina (grand-mother of Cousin Tabitha Twitchit) — died of a thimble in a Christmas plum-pudding. *I* never put any article of metal in *my* puddings or pies."

Duchess looked aghast, and tilted up the pie-dish.

"I have only four patty-pans, and they are all in the cupboard."

Duchess set up a howl.

"I shall die! I shall die! I have swallowed a patty-pan! Oh, my dear Ribby, I do feel so ill!"

"IT is impossible, my dear Duchess; there was not a patty-pan."

Duchess moaned and whined and rocked herself about.

"Oh I feel so dreadful, I have swallowed a patty-pan!"

"There was *nothing* in the pie," said Ribby severely.

"Yes there *was*, my dear Ribby, I am sure I have swallowed it!"

"LET me prop you up with a pillow, my dear
Duchess; where do you think you feel it?"

"Oh I do feel so ill *all over* me, my dear Ribby;
I have swallowed a large tin patty-pan with a
sharp scalloped edge!"

"Shall I run for the doctor? I will just lock up
the spoons!"

"Oh yes, yes! fetch Dr. Maggotty, my dear Ribby;
he is a Pie himself, he will certainly understand."

RIBBY settled Duchess in an armchair before the fire, and went out and hurried to the village to look for the doctor.

She found him at the smithy.

He was occupied in putting rusty nails into a bottle of ink, which he had obtained at the post office.

"Gammon? ha! HA!" said he, with his head on one side.

Ribby explained that her guest had swallowed a patty-pan.

"Spinach? ha! HA!" said he, and accompanied her with alacrity.

HE hopped so fast that Ribby had to run. It was most conspicuous. All the village could see that Ribby was fetching the doctor.

"I *knew* they would over-eat themselves!" said Cousin Tabitha Twitchit.

But while Ribby had been hunting for the doctor — a curious thing had happened to Duchess, who had been left by herself, sitting before the fire, sighing and groaning and feeling very unhappy.

"How *could* I have swallowed it! such a large thing as a patty-pan!"

She got up and went to the table, and felt inside the pie-dish again with a spoon.

"No; there is no patty-pan, and I put one in; and nobody has eaten pie except me, so I must have swallowed it!"

SHE sat down again, and stared mournfully at the grate. The fire crackled and danced, and something sizz-z-zled!

Duchess started! She opened the door of the *top* oven; out came a rich steamy flavour of veal and ham, and there stood a fine brown pie — and through a hole in the top of the pie-crust there was a glimpse of a little tin patty-pan!

Duchess drew a long breath —

"THEN I must have been eating MOUSE! . . .
No wonder I feel ill . . . But perhaps I should
feel worse if I had really swallowed a patty-pan!"
Duchess reflected — "What a very awkward thing
to have to explain to Ribby! I think I will put
my pie in the back-yard and say nothing about it.
When I go home, I will run round and take it away."

SHE put it outside the back door, and sat down again by the fire, and shut her eyes; when Ribby arrived with the doctor, she seemed fast asleep.

"Gammon, ha, HA?" said the doctor.

"I am feeling very much better," said Duchess, waking up with a jump.

"I am truly glad to hear it! He has brought you a pill, my dear Duchess!"

"I think I should feel *quite* well if he only felt my pulse," said Duchess, backing away from the magpie, who sidled up with something in his beak.

"It is only a bread-pill, you had much better take it; drink a little milk, my dear Duchess!"

"Gammon? Gammon?" said the doctor, while Duchess coughed and choked.

"DON'T say that again!" said Ribby, losing her temper—"Here, take this bread and jam, and get out into the yard!"

"Gammon and Spinach! ha ha HA!" shouted Dr. Maggotty triumphantly outside the back door . . .

"I am feeling very much better, my dear Ribby," said Duchess. "Do you not think that I had better go home before it gets dark?"

"Perhaps it might be wise, my dear Duchess. I will lend you a nice warm shawl, and you shall take my arm."

"I would not trouble you for worlds; I feel wonderfully better. One pill of Dr. Maggotty —"

"Indeed it is most admirable, if it has cured you of a patty-pan! I will call directly after breakfast to ask how you have slept."

RIBBY and Duchess said goodbye affectionately, and Duchess started home. Half-way up the lane she stopped and looked back; Ribby had gone in and shut her door. Duchess slipped through the fence, and ran round to the back of Ribby's house and peeped into the yard.

Upon the roof of the pig-stye sat Dr. Maggotty and three jackdaws. The jackdaws were eating pie-crust, and the magpie was drinking gravy out of a patty-pan.

"Gammon, ha, HA!" he shouted when he saw Duchess's little black nose peeping round the corner.

Duchess ran home feeling uncommonly silly!

When Ribby came out for a pailful of water to wash up the tea-things, she found a pink and white pie-dish lying smashed in the middle of the yard.

THE patty-pan was under the pump, where Dr. Maggotty had considerately left it.

Ribby stared with amazement — "Did you ever see the like! so there really *was* a patty-pan? . . . But *my* patty-pans are all in the kitchen cupboard. Well I never did! . . . Next time I want to give a party — I will invite Cousin Tabitha Twitchit!"